Beautiful Princess Tori greets the guests at the palace.

King Frederic and Duchess Amelia are hosting a royal reception.

Everyone is excited about Meribella's five hundredth anniversary celebration.

Princess Trevi and Princess Meredith curtsy for their guests.

Vanessa is Princess Tori's pampered pet.

Princess Tori and her sisters love playing tricks.

Duchess Amelia gets a big surprise!

Keira is the world's biggest pop star.

Keira's dancers get the crowd excited.

Keira performs at many concerts.

Keira's puppy, Riff, is her best friend.

Sometimes Keira wishes she weren't a pop star.

Crider is Keira's greedy manager.

Princess Tori wishes she could be a pop star like Keira.

Vanessa tries a pop-star move!

Keira wishes she could be a princess like Tori.

Riff is doggone cute!

Vanessa and Riff become good friends, too!

Princess Tori uses her magical hairbrush to create a sparkling new hairstyle.

Keira uses her magical microphone to transform her clothes into a glamorous gown.

Vanessa and Riff are amazed by the magic!

Princess Tori transforms into Keira!

Keira transforms into Princess Tori.

Keira and Tori can't believe how much they look like one another!

Tori shows Keira Meribella's secret garden.
It contains the Diamond Gardenia.
It gives the kingdom life.

Garden fairies guard the diamond plant.

The garden fairies use a tiny diamond to make a star necklace for Keira.

They use a tiny diamond to make a heart necklace for Tori. The girls are best friends forever.

Crider spies the Diamond Gardenia and plans to steal it!

The girls decide to switch places. Princess Tori learns to dance like a pop star.

Vanessa and Riff are *pup* stars!

Keira loves to dance, dance, dance!

Keira's dancers can't wait to perform!

Princess Tori gets to sing all of Keira's hit songs at rehearsal.

This royal horse is beautiful.

Keira has fun being a princess.

Tori calls Keira.

The girls are having so much fun that they decide to not switch back yet.

During dance rehearsal, Princess Tori learns that it's not easy walking in someone else's shoes.

Keira's dancers can't understand why the star is having trouble.

Keira, as the princess, has tea at the palace.

Princess Trevi and Princess Meredith wonder why their sister isn't acting like herself.

Princess Tori takes a walk through the kingdom.

Keira's fans think Tori is Keira and ask for her autograph.

Princess fun!

Keira is happy and writes a new song.

Keira's concert is about to begin—but where is Keira?

Princess Tori is nervous about performing. When she sings, though, the crowd loves her!

Crider steals the diamonds!

Crider's henchman, Rupert, pulls up the Diamond Gardenia.

Princess Tori notices the leaves begin to fade.
She switches back to herself.

Keira changes back to herself, too. She sets out to find Crider and get the Diamond Gardenia.

Princess Tori sees Crider getting away in a carriage.

Keira decides she and Tori must ride a makeshift zip line down the hill to stop Crider.

Princess Tori stops the carriage!

Keira recovers the magic diamonds from Crider.

The two friends replant the diamond plant—
but it is too late!

Tori remembers their necklaces and plants them. Two new Diamond Gardenias sprout!

The kingdom is saved!
Vanessa, Riff, and the fairies celebrate!

Tori realizes she likes being a princess.
Keira realizes she likes being a pop star.
They decide to stay as themselves.